OCT 2001

The Wolf of Gubbio

Story by Michael Bedard
Paintings by Murray Kimber

Stoddart Kids
TORONTO • NEW YORK

NORTHPORT PUBLIC LIBRARY
NORTHPORT, NEW YORK

For Kathryn.
— M.B.
For my wife, Kari, and the little one en route.
— M.K.

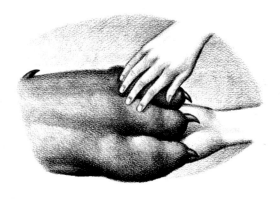

Text copyright © 2000 by Michael Bedard
Illustrations copyright © 2000 by Murray Kimber

All rights reserved. No part of this publication may be
reproduced or transmitted in any form or by any means,
electronic or mechanical, including photocopying, recording,
or any information storage and retrieval system, without
permission in writing from the publisher.

Published in Canada in 2000 by
Stoddart Kids,
a division of Stoddart Publishing Co. Limited
34 Lesmill Road
Toronto, ON M3B 2T6
Tel (416) 445-3333 Fax (416) 445-5967
E-mail cservice@genpub.com

Distributed in Canada by
General Distribution Services
325 Humber College Blvd.,
Toronto, ON M9W 7C3
Tel (416) 213-1919 Fax (416) 213-1917
E-mail cservice@genpub.com

Published in the United States in 2001 by
Stoddart Kids,
a division of Stoddart Publishing Co. Limited
180 Varick Street, 9th Floor
New York, New York 10014
Toll free 1-800-805-1083
E-mail gdsinc@genpub.com

Distributed in the United States by
General Distribution Services
4500 Witmer Industrial Estates, PMB 128
Niagara Falls, New York 14305-1386
Toll free 1-800-805-1083
E-mail gdsinc@genpub.com

Canadian Cataloguing in Publication Data

Bedard, Michael, 1949–
The wolf of Gubbio

ISBN 0-7737-3250-0

1. Francis, of Assisi, Saint, 1182–1226 – Legends.   I. Kimber, Murray, 1964–
II. Title.

PS8553.E298W64 2000   j398.22   C00-931095-9
PZ8.1.B3888Wo 2000

THE CANADA COUNCIL | LE CONSEIL DES ARTS
FOR THE ARTS | DU CANADA
SINCE 1957 | DEPUIS 1957

*We acknowledge for their financial support of our
publishing program the Canada Council, the Ontario Arts
Council, and the Government of Canada through the
Book Publishing Industry Development Program (BPIDP).*

*When a wolf terrorizes the town of Gubbio, a humble stranger
confronts the beast and makes peace between it and the villagers.
Based on one of the St. Francis of Assisi legends.*

Printed and bound in Hong Kong, China
by Book Art Inc. Toronto

It is near noon in Gubbio. I sit at the window of the house and look down the narrow lane, where the great grey wolf goes from door to door. Other faces watch at other windows. Soon the wolf will come to our door as well. But I am not afraid, for I have seen a wonder in Gubbio.

Ours is a mountain town. The streets are steep and narrow, the houses made of stone. Around the town there stands a wall.

Once we lived in fear. The gates were locked and barred. Those who left the town, left armed with pikes and pitchforks, and traveled in groups for safety. Many were afraid to leave at all.

For in a cave in the woods below the town there lived a monstrous wolf. And when hunger drew him from his den, so fierce was he that no living thing was safe from him.

"Two more sheep were carried off in the night," said Father, returning from the fields one day. "It is the wolf's work. Who is safe against a creature such as this?"

At night we lay in bed and listened to the howl of the wolf on the hill. In sleep, we saw his shadow slink along the moonlit wall as the great beast circled the town.

Then one day a ragged band of strangers appeared. They were barefoot, their coarse robes belted at the waist with cord. Whispers followed them as they walked along the cobbled lanes.

"It is the Poverello," I heard someone say. "The little poor one. He calls all creatures brother and sister. They say he understands the language of bird and beast."

"Some say he works wonders," said another.

He did not look like a wonder worker. But there was something in his eyes when they met my gaze that made me follow with the others as he moved through the town.

He sat down by the well in the square, drew water, drank, and passed the cup to his companions. He spoke quietly with the crowd that had gathered there. The talk soon turned to the wolf who terrorized the town.

The Poverello listened intently to the story they had to tell. When they were done he quietly rose and said, "I will go to see this wolf."

"No!" the people pleaded. "You will surely be killed."

"Nonetheless, I shall go," he said.

He made his way to the town gates with his companions following at a distance behind. And behind them further still, those of the townsfolk who dared to go. I went with them and saw all with my own eyes, or I would not believe it to be true.

We walked down the path that led into the woods. There, in the shadows of the tall oaks and walnut trees, the wolf had his lair.

All about the path was strewn with bones. At the sight of them, all but the bravest held back and watched as the little brother went on alone.

Suddenly there came a fearful howl, and out from the shadows
sprang the wolf. At the sight of him the people turned and ran.
I climbed up into the closest tree and cowered there. But the little
brother walked on. With jaws agape, the great beast bounded
toward him.

And then I saw a thing I thought impossible. For as the wolf was
about to pounce, the brother raised his hand and made a sign of
blessing.

"Brother Wolf," he said. "I command you in the name of God to
harm neither me nor any other."

The wolf stopped as if he had been struck. He closed his great
mouth and came walking to where the little brother stood.

"Brother Wolf," said the Poverello, "you have done great wrong to kill the creatures of God. The people of Gubbio cry out against you and would have you hanged on the gallows like a criminal. But I wish to make peace between you and them. If they forgive the ill you have done, you in turn, must promise to offend no more."

The wolf inclined his head and wagged his tail as if to say he understood and agreed.

"I know it is hunger that has driven you to do these wicked deeds. Pledge to me that you will keep peace, and I promise you will hunger no more."

At this, the Poverello held out his hand, and I watched as the wolf raised his great paw and placed it gently in the brother's palm.

The Poverello turned then, and walked back toward the town with the wolf following close behind. As they went beneath the tree where I hid, the wolf looked up at me.

Through the city gates and up the cobbled streets the strange
procession passed. And all the townsfolk marveled at the fierce
beast become mild as a lamb.

They gathered in the square. The little brother sat down by the well with his companions and gave the wolf to drink. Then he spoke to the people.

"Friends," he said, "put away your fear. Brother Wolf has pledged to keep peace with you. It was hunger that drove him to these evil deeds. Do you, for your part, promise to feed him faithfully each day?"

With one accord the people promised to provide for the wolf and to welcome him among them without fear.

Then the brother turned to the wolf and said, "Brother Wolf, pledge me your faith again, before these people, that you will keep the promise you have made."

While all the town looked on, the wolf raised his ragged paw and placed it in the brother's palm.

And so it was done. From that day to this, the wolf has lived within these walls. He freely wanders field and lane, and even the dogs do not think to bark at him.

Each day at noon he goes from door to door, doing harm to none nor fearing harm. Soon he will come to our door.

I will give him this food we have set aside for him. And when he is done, he will hold his paw out to me, and I will take it in my hand.

The story of the wolf of Gubbio is one of the legends of St.
Francis of Assisi. Francis was the son of a wealthy cloth merchant.
When he was nineteen, as the result of a vision, he renounced his
family's riches and embraced a life dedicated to poverty. He and
his followers wandered from town to town through Italy, preach-
ing the gospel of brotherly love and caring for the poor and sick.
He was known among the people as the *Poverello*.

Francis felt that all of Nature was the mirror of God and called all
creatures his brothers and sisters. After his death in 1226, many
legends surrounding his life were collected and written down. The
story of the wolf of Gubbio first appeared in a collection called
the *Fioretti* (The Little Flowers).

One wonders sometimes, whether stories such as this could really
be true. According to the legend, the wolf lived at peace among
the people of Gubbio for two years and then died of old age. In
the year 1873, when workers in the town of Gubbio were repair-
ing a chapel dedicated to St. Francis, they raised up one of the
flagstones on the floor. Buried beneath it they discovered the skull
of a large wolf.

398.22   Bedard, Michael.
BED
          The wolf of Gubbio.

$15.95

DATE			

OCT   2001

NORTHPORT-EAST NORTHPORT
PUBLIC LIBRARY
151 Laurel Avenue
Northport, NY 11768

BAKER & TAYLOR